PAWTUCKET PUBLIC LIBRARY

DISCARD
WITHDRA
PAWTUCKET PUBLIC LIBRARY

P9-DXT-076
3 1218 00429 2158

DUE

AUG 0 7 2014   MAY 17 2017   MAY 17 2017
MAR 2 1 2018   2013
SI OCT 3 0 2014   MAY 17 2017   010
S   2014
JAN 2 7 2015   6 2013
FEB 2 0 2016   MAY 2 0 2019

MAR 0 3 2015   JUL 1 0 2010
JUL 2 7 2015   AUG 2 6 2010
MAR 3 1 2016   SEP 1 3 2010
NOV 1 0 2015
JAN 0 4 2017   SEP 2 9 2010
FEB 1 5 2017

OCT 2 5 2010

DISCARD
WITHDRAW
....
PAWTUCKET PUBLIC LIBRARY

KAY THOMPSON'S ELOISE

Eloise Throws a Party!

STORY BY **Lisa McClatchy**

ILLUSTRATED BY **Tammie Lyon**

Ready-to-Read
Aladdin
NEW YORK · LONDON · TORONTO · SYDNEY

ALADDIN PAPERBACKS
An imprint of Simon & Schuster Children's Publishing Division
1230 Avenue of the Americas, New York, NY 10020
Copyright © 2008 by the Estate of Kay Thompson
All rights reserved, including the right of reproduction in whole or in part in any form.
"Eloise" and related marks are trademarks of the Estate of Kay Thompson.
READY-TO-READ, ALADDIN PAPERBACKS, and related logo are
registered trademarks of Simon & Schuster, Inc.
The text of this book was set in Century Old Style.
Manufactured in the United States of America
First Aladdin Paperbacks edition May 2008
2 4 6 8 10 9 7 5 3 1
Library of Congress Control Number 2007938994
ISBN-13: 978-1-4169-6172-7
ISBN-10: 1-4169-6172-0

3 1218 00429 2158

My name is Eloise.
I am a city child.

I have a dog.

He is a pug.

His name is Weenie.
Today is Weenie's birthday.

I have a big
surprise for Weenie.
I am throwing him a party!

Nanny is helping me surprise Weenie.

"Oh Nanny!" I say.
"Weenie and I are
   going for our walk now!"

I give Nanny a big wink.
She gives me the A-OK.

Weenie and I walk to
Central Park.

We say hello to all
our horse friends.

Weenie sniffs the flowers
I pick him a bouquet.

we get back,
manager says,
y birthday, Weenie!"

He hands me a box.
"For Weenie," he whispers
to me.

I give him the A-OK.

When we get to
our apartment,

Nanny yells,
"Surprise, Weenie!"
I yell,
"Surprise, Weenie!"

Room Service yells,
"Surprise, Weenie!"

The doorman yells,
"Surprise, Weenie!"

The dogs bark,
"Surprise, Weenie!"

"Look, Weenie," I say.

"It's Mr. Afghan Hound
from the twelfth floor!"

for
Leenie

"And Spot, the firemen's dalmatian! And Priscilla Poodle!"

"And Doxy,
the manager's
dachshund!"

We all dance around.

Then Weenie and his friends
gobble up doggy biscuits
and bonbons.

Weenie tries to eat the candles on his doggy cake.

He plays
tug-of-war

with his new
doggy toy.

I help Weenie
open his presents.
Weenie plays with
more doggy toys!

Then I give
Weenie my present.

"It is a sweater, Weenie,"
I say.

Then we all curl up
on my bed

and take a good,
long doggy nap.

Oh, I love, love,
love birthdays!